Cale the Corgi and the Cranky Bull

ISBN 978-1-0980-4079-6 (paperback)
ISBN 978-1-0980-4080-2 (digital)

Christian Faith Publishing, Inc.
832 Park Avenue
Meadville, PA 16335
www.christianfaithpublishing.com

Printed in the United States of America

Book 2

Cale the Corgi
and the
Cranky Bull

H.M. Stryker

Cale the corgi lived on a farm with her human, Mr. Dale K. Harm. One bright sunny day Mr. Harm went with his stock trailer to the town known as Kent. The farm animals wondered, when they heard the news, just what Mr. Harm was going to do.

"I know what's up," Hip-Hop Horse neighed. "He's going to buy us all some more hay."

"No, that's not it," Pearl Pig declared. "He went to pick us pigs up some fake hair."

"Why would he do that?" Clarice Cow questioned.

Pearl shrugged. "It was just a suggestion."

"He took the trailer with him," said Cale. "I'll bet he went to a livestock sale."

Cale was right, for Mr. Harm went to a livestock sale at the sale barn in Kent. The farmer wanted to buy a new bull. A Black Angus with papers he was hoping to pull home in the trailer and be a friend to his cows. He just hoped the price wouldn't be "Oh, golly-wow!"

And later that day home Mr. Harm came with a bull and a few thousand dollars less to his name.

The other animals—Cale and friends—all gathered 'round to make their wonderings end. With bated breath they watched and waited, with each passing second growing elated. Just what had Mr. Harm brought home from the sale?

Maybe some more cows, sheep, or goats, thought Cale.

And then the moment they'd all waited for came. Mr. Harm opened the trailer and called out a name.

"Come on, Danny. Come on out, boy. You're going to like it here—you'll jump for joy!"

And out of the trailer came a surprise—the biggest bull on which the friends had ever set eyes!

He was blacker than black, a moonless night cloaked in soot. He was seven feet tall from his head to his foot. A big hump on his neck and muscles so big and tight, this bull looked like he was ready to fight. The gleam in his eyes said loud and clear, "Don't mess with me. I'll kick your rear!"

Cale and friends all stared in awe. Good golly jeepers, was this guy an outlaw? "Oh my goodness!" Clarice exclaimed. "Forget Danny, Bruiser would be a much better name!"

Hip-Hop added, "I wouldn't want to feel his wrath. I think we should all stay out of his path."

The friends all agreed and watched as Danny Bull was let out to pasture. Something told Cale this would be a disaster.

Two days later Cale was making her rounds when she spotted Clarice. She looked a bit down.

"What's wrong, Clarice?" Cale asked. "You look so sad."

The Angus sniffled, "Oh, Cale, it's that new bull. He really *is* big and bad. He picks on me and calls me names."

"Why's that?"

"It's my hair bow. He says it makes me fair game."

Cale was stunned and stood there in shock. How on earth could Clarice be being mocked? Clarice was the sweetest, funniest, friendliest cow, and for someone to bully her? That had to stop *now*!

With a growl and a snarl, Cale about faced. Time to put this new Danny Bull in his place! Her head held high and her stubbed tail up too, Cale marched her way through the morning dew. There before her, the bull stood a little bit off from the herd.

"Hey, Danny," Cale yapped. "Can I have a word?"

The Black Angus beast raised his great head, and rather than answering, he laughed instead.

"A word with you?" Danny Bull snorted.

"You see any other dog asking?" Cale retorted.

"No, I don't. In fact, all I see is a short, fat little mutt standing right before me. What happened to your legs, poochie? They're nearly half gone. And what of your tail? Tail chasing gone wrong? Are you even sure you're a dog and not some overgrown varmint?"

That was a joke, but there was no charm in it.

Cale wouldn't lie, Danny's comments stung. But Clarice needed help, and Cale wasn't done.

"Danny, I'm here to ask you to cease your bullying of my good friend Clarice. What harm has she ever done you? She's everyone's friend and could be yours too, if only you'd stop being so mean and were nicer—"

"I've heard enough!" Danny cut in. "Get out of my pasture!"

"But—" Cale began. Then Danny charged, and the poor corgi ran. Her little legs blurred and paws pounded the ground, and so did the bull's hooves as he tried running her down. Under the fence Cale darted with just seconds to spare!

Danny bellowed, and snorted, and pawed at the air.

"Take this as a warning, dog!" the bull did shout. "My pasture, my turf. You need to stay out. And as for your little cow friend, ain't my fault she's weak."

Cale wanted to snap back but turned the other cheek. Fighting with Danny would get her nowhere. The little dog knew this, but it still wasn't fair! Clarice needed help, this much was certain. But so far all of Cale's ideas just were not working. So with a heavy sigh and aching feet, the corgi walked away, accepting defeat.

Later on Cale and friends all went for a walk, and after some silence, they started to talk.

"I'm sorry, Clarice," Cale apologized. "I just couldn't make him see eye to eye."

"It's okay, Cale," Clarice mooed. "Danny's just a big rude bully with a bad attitude. His bullying hurts, but I'll just learn to ignore it."

"You shouldn't have to," Cale insisted. "There's no excuse for it! One way or another that bull's getting a piece of my mind."

"But how?" Pearl asked. "He nearly kicked your behind!"

"Cale," Hip-Hop chimed in, "Danny tried to run you into the ground!"

"I know," Cale agreed, "but I can't let Clarice down! Danny might be big and harsh and say hurtful stuff, but we *need* to stand up to him. Enough is enough!"

Hip-Hop asked, "But how do we bring his bullying to an end?"

Cale smirked and replied, "With the help of some friends." And with that Cale began hatching an idea that was downright brilliant and smashing.

The very next day as the sun rose into the sky, old Danny Bull was in for a surprise. Without so much as a whimper or even a flinch, Cale crawled right under the fence. Head high and determined, Cale marched out into the field. She would not turn tail. She would not yield. The pup went right up to the bull and looked him in the eye, and with a defiant smile, she greeted him.

"Hi."

Danny pawed the ground, snorted, and glared. "I thought I told you to stay out!" he declared.

Cale just looked at him and gave a big grin. "You did," she assured him, "but let me begin. First of all, the pasture's not yours, it's Mr. Harm's. And everyone shares it here on the farm. Second, indulge me if you will, please. We need to talk about my good friend Clarice."

Danny Bull snorted. "The cow with the hair bow?"

"Yes," Cale answered. "She's a bit low. You pick on and bully her, and that isn't right."

"I'm a bull," Danny said, "and bulls want to fight."

"I know," Cale nodded, still standing her ground. "But bulls usually fight when there are other bulls around. You're the only one here, so there's no reason to fight."

The bull thought this fact over before nodding. "All right. I see your point now. You've made it quite clear."

Our dear little corgi now had the bull's ear.

"Now, I know that you're big, strong, and intimidating. But by being a bully, you really are limiting your chances to make friends and be pals with others."

As she said this, the farm animals gathered 'round, one after another.

"What do you mean I don't have friends?" Danny demanded. "Of course, I do!"

"No," said Clarice, "not really. We're all just scared of you."

"You walk around and bully everyone," another cow said. "You throw your weight around and throw up your head."

"Well, what else can I do?" Danny asked. "If I can be frank, I'm new on this farm and need to establish my rank."

"Establishing rank," Pearl pointed out, "is well enough."
Hip-Hop came in. "But, dude, you're being too rough."
"If you're just a big bully," Cale said, "no one will
respect you. They'll just be scared of and even detest
you. Danny, you make friends by being nice and kind.
If you're those two things we'll all have peace of mind."

For a long time Danny was quiet as he thought this over—and over and over and over and over. Were Cale and her friends right about him being a bully? The bull thought back and remembered wholly how mean he had been to everyone here—some of the herd; Cale; and poor Clarice, who he'd brought to tears. For the very first time, Danny realized just how rude and despicable he'd been to these guys.

In the blink of an eye, the bull felt sorrow and shame. He had to do something to better his name. Bashful and sheepish, Danny looked in their eyes.

"Oh, gosh," he murmured, "I'm sorry, you guys. I know what I did was mean and was wrong. It's just that I haven't really had friends in so long. I've been sold and been bought so many times, and at a new place, I can get out of line. A new farm can be daunting, even for a bull. And sometimes my nerves will take control. But I'm really sorry for bullying. I mean that, I do. And you're the first ones to make me see that. Thank you. And I'm sorry, Clarice, for making fun of your bow."

Clarice smiled and said, "Eh, we'll let it go."

And from that day on, Danny the Bull got rid of his bad attitude and meanness in full. That day, Cale and friends made clear one rule: Don't be a bully. It's really not cool.

About the Author

Born and raised in central Nebraska, H. M. Stryker has lived the "farm-girl life" to almost the fullest extent of the term. She is an avid animal lover who has owned and raised many pets, in both the generic and not so generic sense of the word. That's where she draws much of her inspiration for children's books from, the main source of which happens to be the family Corgi,: Pudge. You thought the name was going to be "Cale", didn't you?

Ms. Stryker first developed an interest in story-telling and writing in her pre-teens, and has been working on her craft since. She tries to write something every day, even if it's just a sentence or two. And if, sometimes, she can't even manage to accomplish that… well, it's the thought that counts. "With writing, practice might not ever make perfect," she claims, "but is sure does make it better."

When not writing, working, or helping on her family's farm, Stryker can be found participating in her community's thespian group and different local choral activities. She also enjoys helping with the One Acts program at her old high school. However, her favorite pastime is still spending time with and caring for animals of all sizes and shapes. "My life wouldn't be half as interesting without them," Stryker says. "Neither would my writing. It's a good thing animals don't demand to be kept out of books."

CPSIA information can be obtained
at www.ICGtesting.com
Printed in the USA
LVHW070801191220
674217LV00014B/615

9 781098 040796